Photo courtesy of Mary Swanson

The actual Nosey the Elephant. Always curious and affectionate, Nosey would stretch her trunk to greet her loving fans or receive a tasty peanut.

"**N**osey the Elephant" is a story based on fact. She came by ship in 1949 as the last load of Thai elephants sold in the United States. Nosey lived at the zoo for 44 years and died in 1993.

Today, no animals are taken from the wild for zoos. Zoo keepers cannot work freely with elephants. For safety, the elephants are restrained or separated by bars.

I dedicate this book to
Robby, Joshua, Kendall, and Zachary

In Memory of
Doc Chaffee
who was the
inspiration
for all these
stories

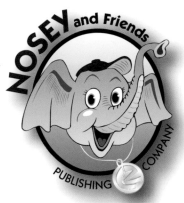

The story "Nosey the Elephant" is an imprint of Nosey and Friends Publishing Co.
Published by Nosey and Friends Publishing Co.
5647 N. Prospect
Fresno, CA 93711
Copyright © 2003 Jean Chaffee
Fresno, California
All rights reserved.
Printed in Korea

Fourth Printing / 2M

Library of Congress Control Number: 2004090453
Jean Chaffee
The story of "Nosey the Elephant" / written by Jean Chaffee
Illustrated by Ernie "Hergie" Hergenroeder
Summary: The story of children working together collecting dimes, nickels
& quarters to buy an elephant for the town zoo.
ISBN: 0-9748075-0-8 (Hardcover)
Copyright to include all characters, design & story concept.

NOSEY The Elephant

by
Jean Chaffee

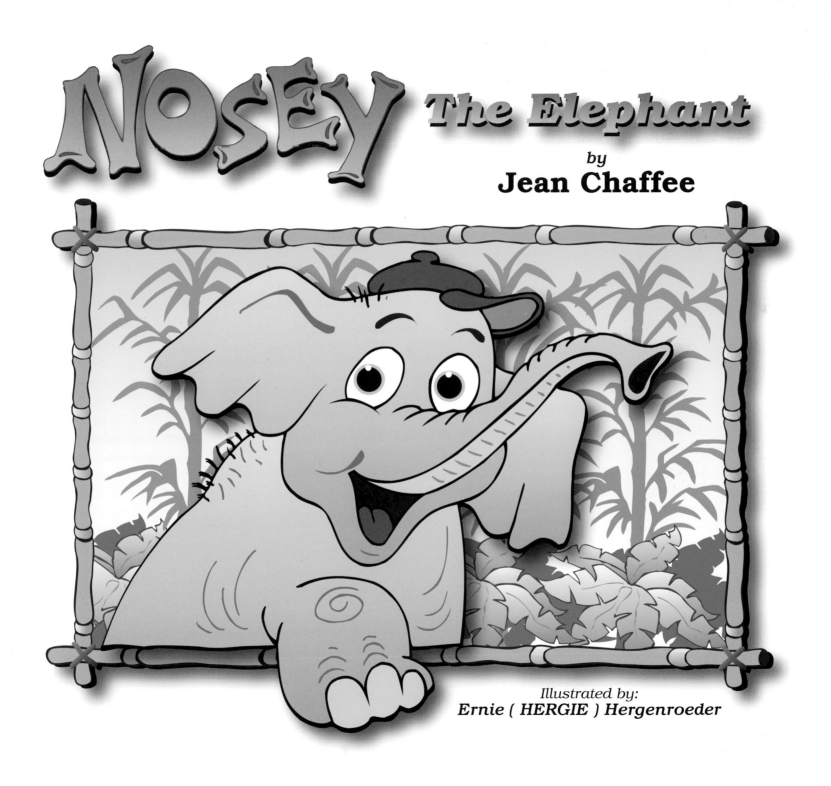

Illustrated by:
Ernie (HERGIE) Hergenroeder

A long time ago, Nosey lived in a small village in Thailand. She lived with her mother, her sisters, aunties, and cousins.
Her mother worked hard carrying big logs from the rain forest.

1

Nosey walked beside her mother as she worked. The Mahout
taught her to follow directions. "I want to grow up to be just
like my mother," said Nosey. She was very happy.

One day several men took Nosey and her friends away. The young elephants were put on a ship going to America. It was going to be a very long journey. Nosey was sad because she missed her mother.

When they were far out at sea, a big storm appeared. The wind blew and it got very dark. Nosey cried because it was so scary. The ship tossed and turned, and Nosey got seasick. After many hours, the storm went away and Nosey was safe again.

Finally, the ship arrived in America. The elephants went to a farm to wait for their new home. Nosey waited and waited.

Her friends went away to different zoos and she was very lonesome. "I wonder where I am going to go," worried Nosey.

5

The children in Fresno heard about the lonely elephant. They saved their allowance to give to the zoo. They sold lemonade. They made elephant cookies to sell to their neighbors. They had to raise $3500 to buy the elephant.

6

The children took their jars full of dimes, nickels, and quarters to the zookeeper. He said,"Now there is enough money to buy the elephant!"
The zoo held a "Name the Elephant" contest, and the children sent in their names.
The zookeeper chose the name, "Nosey."

FRESNO ZOO

Help NAME Fresno's new
ELEPHANT
contest

7

On a beautiful September day, Nosey got into a truck for a drive to her new home. She arrived just as the parade was ready to start. Hundreds of people stood on the sidewalks to see Nosey. They were very excited.

The truck stopped in front of the Water Tower. The zookeepers backed Nosey out of the truck. As she turned to face the people, they began to cheer and call her name.

Nosey! Nosey! Nosey! But all the noise made her very nervous.

Her zookeeper rubbed her trunk and gave her some apples. They whispered nice things in her ear. Finally she calmed down and got ready for the parade. People threw peanuts and flowers as they welcomed Nosey.

Nosey led the grand parade down the main street.
She held her head high as she greeted her new friends.

12

A big horse walked by in the parade. She had never seen a horse before. She twirled around and lifted her trunk high in the air. She let out a big scream as the mothers rushed their children out of the way. The zookeeper grabbed hold of Nosey to keep her from running away.

At the end of the parade it was time to take Nosey to the zoo. The zookeeper led her to the truck but she refused to get in. She stomped her foot; she shook her head, **"NO"**! **"No more boats and no more trucks"**, said Nosey.

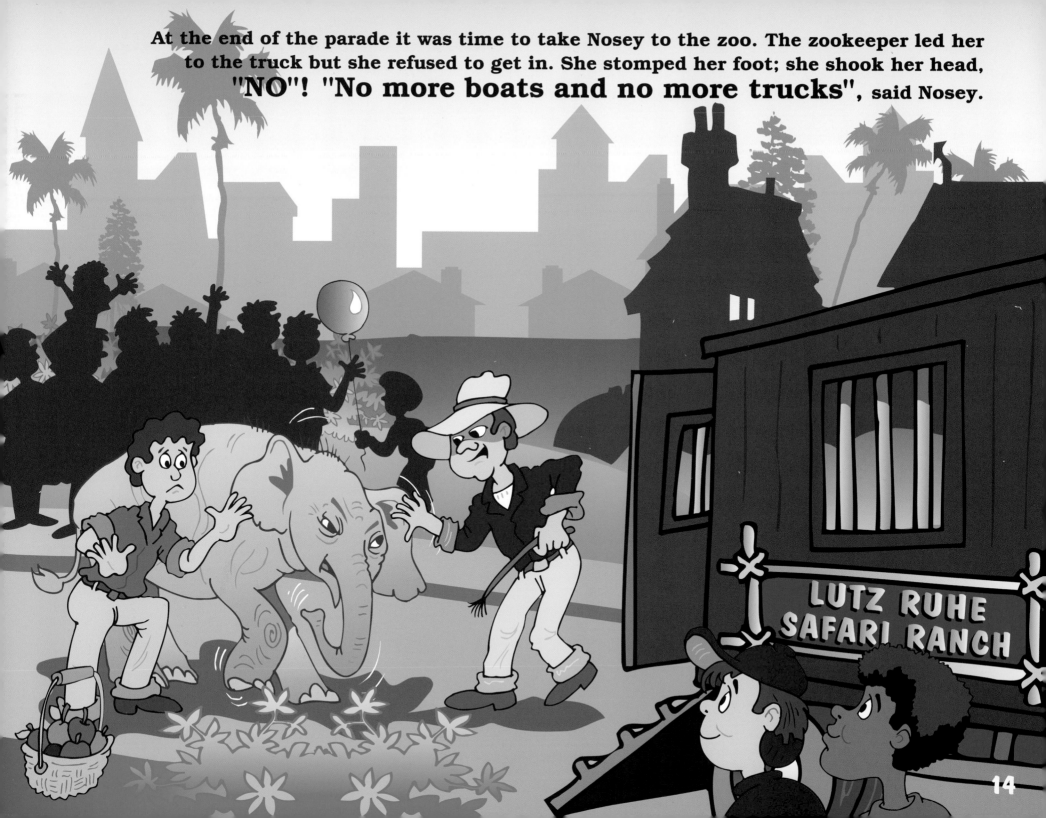

The zookeeper pushed and pulled. He tempted her with carrots, but Nosey still said, **"NO."** Nosey was so big that the zookeepers couldn't move her. Soon the zookeeper shrugged his shoulders and said, "OK, let's walk to the zoo."

Nosey and her zookeepers started walking.
They turned around and saw all the people walking behind them.
The people laughed and danced as they walked to the zoo.
Nosey was very happy.

16

A pile of carrots, a bucket of peanuts, and fresh water greeted Nosey in her new home. She was tired and thirsty after her long walk. She filled her trunk with water. Then she looked at the people and said to herself, "I am going to play a joke on everyone."

Nosey used her trunk to spray the water on all the people. They laughed because Nosey had surprised them. This was Nosey's new home and she liked her new friends. She said, "I am very, very happy because I have lots of friends now."

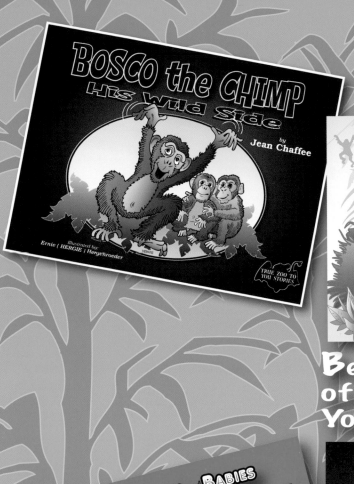

BOSCO the CHIMP
His Wild Side
by Jean Chaffee
Illustrated by: Ernie (HERGIE) Hergenroeder
TRUE ZOO TO YOU STORIES

AZAK
Learns to Read
by Jean Chaffee
Illustrated by: Ernie Hergenroeder "HERGIE"
TRUE ZOO TO YOU STORIES

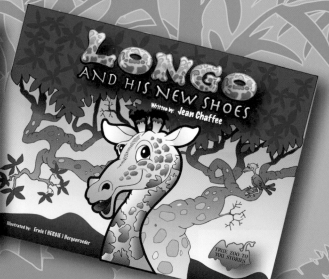

MOJA THE LION
Goes To The Dentist
by Jean Chaffee
Illustrated by: Ernie Hergenroeder "HERGIE"
TRUE ZOO TO YOU STORIES

Be sure to collect all of these "True Zoo To You Stories".

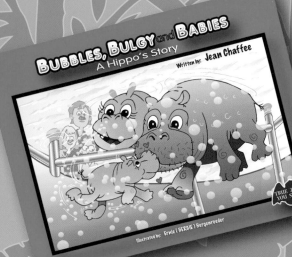

BUBBLES, BULGY and BABIES
A Hippo's Story
Written by: Jean Chaffee
Illustrated by: Ernie (HERGIE) Hergenroeder
TRUE ZOO TO YOU STORIES

NOSEY'S BIG MOVE
by Jean Chaffee
Illustrated by: Ernie (HERGIE) Hergenroeder
TRUE ZOO TO YOU STORIES

LONGO
AND HIS NEW SHOES
Written by: Jean Chaffee
Illustrated by: Ernie (HERGIE) Hergenroeder
TRUE ZOO TO YOU STORIES